PENNY DRAWS
A FIRST CRUSH

ALSO BY SARA SHEPARD

Penny Draws a Best Friend
Penny Draws a School Play
Penny Draws a Secret Adventure
Penny Draws a Class Trip
Penny Draws a Team Sport

PENNY DRAWS
A FIRST CRUSH

SARA SHEPARD

G. P. PUTNAM'S SONS

G. P. PUTNAM'S SONS
An imprint of Penguin Random House LLC
1745 Broadway, New York, New York 10019

Produced by Alloy Entertainment
30 Hudson Yards, 22nd floor • New York, NY 10001

First published in the United States of America by G. P. Putnam's Sons,
an imprint of Penguin Random House LLC, 2025

Copyright © 2025 by Sara Shepard and Alloy Entertainment LLC

Penguin Random House values and supports copyright. Copyright fuels creativity, encourages diverse voices, promotes free speech, and creates a vibrant culture. Thank you for buying an authorized edition of this book and for complying with copyright laws by not reproducing, scanning, or distributing any part of it in any form without permission. You are supporting writers and allowing Penguin Random House to continue to publish books for every reader. Please note that no part of this book may be used or reproduced in any manner for the purpose of training artificial intelligence technologies or systems.

G. P. Putnam's Sons is a registered trademark of Penguin Random House LLC.
The Penguin colophon is a registered trademark of Penguin Books Limited.

Visit us online at PenguinRandomHouse.com.

Library of Congress Cataloging-in-Publication Data
Names: Shepard, Sara, 1977- author.
Title: Penny draws a first crush / Sara Shepard.
Description: New York, New York: G. P. Putnam's Sons, 2025. | Series: Penny draws | Audience term: Preteens | Summary: "Penny receives a mysterious note that makes her believe a boy in her class has a crush on her, but she is not quite ready to have a crush on someone just yet"—Provided by publisher.
Identifiers: LCCN 2024036223 (print) | LCCN 2024036224 (ebook) |
ISBN 9780593700341 (hardcover) | ISBN 9780593700358 (epub)
Subjects: CYAC: Diaries—Fiction. | Doodles—Fiction. | Crushes—Fiction. |
Schools—Fiction. | LCGFT: Diary fiction. | Novels.
Classification: LCC PZ7.S54324 Pcf 2025 (print) | LCC PZ7.S54324 (ebook) |
DDC [Fic]—dc23
LC record available at https://lccn.loc.gov/2024036223
LC ebook record available at https://lccn.loc.gov/2024036224

ISBN 9780593700341
1 3 5 7 9 10 8 6 4 2
Manufactured in the United States of America
BVG

Design by Suki Boynton • Text set in Decour

This book is a work of fiction. Any references to historical events, real people, or real places are used fictitiously. Other names, characters, places, and events are products of the author's imagination, and any resemblance to actual events or places or persons, living or dead, is entirely coincidental.

The authorized representative in the EU for product safety and compliance is Penguin Random House Ireland, Morrison Chambers, 32 Nassau Street, Dublin D02 YH68, Ireland, https://eu-contact.penguin.ie.

For Morris!

THE ASSEMBLY

Dear Cosmo,

You probably don't know this, since you're a dog, but I often write my letters to you before I go to sleep. My Feelings Teacher, Mrs. Hines, says that writing stuff down before bed might help me work through everything that happened in the day. That way, my worries won't follow me into my dreams. Or, even worse, keep me awake. Like this.

So that's what I'm doing now—writing to you before I go to bed to work out what happened earlier today.

See, it all started with the announcement my teacher, Miss Kettle, and her hippo puppet, Steve, made just as the morning bell rang.

We all cheered. Assemblies are great because...

1. Our principal, Mr. Mortion, seems boring, but sometimes he can dig up some very interesting guests. Like these:

2. Assemblies take up lots of time in the school day. And it's not just the time spent in the assembly itself—lining up, walking to the multipurpose room, sitting down, and walking back to class take a while, too. Sometimes we get together before the assembly and strategize how to waste the maximum amount of time so we can get out of all kinds of important schoolwork.

3. Assemblies can even be mysterious—like the one today. After lunch, Miss Kettle had us line up and head to the assembly. As we walked, I noticed something strange: All the other kids in the lower grades were still in their classrooms. Why weren't they lining up, too? Then Miss Kettle told us that this particular assembly was for the fifth grade *only*.

We all came up with ideas about why *that* might be.

We walked into the multipurpose room even more anxious and excited. Who was going to talk to us today?

But then, on the stage, I saw someone I recognized.

It was Mrs. Wink, our crossing guard. But what was she doing here?

Mrs. Wink blew her whistle for us to quiet down.

Manners? *Okay...*

I felt confused. We were all supposed to grow up *in two weeks*? That didn't seem like very much time. And did I even *want* to be grown-up?

On second thought, I might not be able to sleep tonight after all.

SHINY PENNY

Dear Cosmo,

When I first opened my eyes this morning, it felt like an ordinary day. I could feel your warm body pressed up against mine. I heard your noisy snores. I also heard the twins, Finn and Fern, crying for Mom to get them out of their cribs to start their baby days.

Then I remembered.

You know, Cosmo, I want to think I've changed a lot since the start of fifth grade. I'm a brand-new Penny. A brand-new *shiny* Penny, maybe. I can handle my worries now. I have good friends who will stick by me even if I *do* struggle with anxiety along the way. And actually, Manners Class didn't come out of the blue—when I thought about it more, I remembered last year's fifth graders taking the class, too. As far as I can tell, all of *them* made it through in one piece.

So I'm trying not to be completely panicked about this whole Manners Class thing. I mean, sure, fifth grade seems *very far* from becoming an adult ... or even a teenager. Also, I'm not sure how important manners even *are*. I mean, my parents don't have good manners every second of the day.

But I'm trying to think positively. Manners Class can't be worse than pickleball. Also, the meetings will be held as a lunch bunch, which means we'll have lunch in a room separate from the cafeteria. That's a huge plus—our school's cafeteria is *so* loud and full of strange smells.

I also talked to my friends about it yesterday over video chat after I wrote my letter to you, Cosmo. We're all on the same page. Manners Class sounds fun, and we aren't going to make that big a deal out of it.

And finally, I talked to my friend Henry from New York City—we met on the special trip to see

Billy J. Plumberry. I asked Henry if *his* school ever had a class where they learned manners.

I asked Henry which flowers meant "You worry too much, but it's okay," but he didn't know.

Anyway, this morning, I got dressed and then went downstairs, trying to be cool and collected. In the kitchen, I saw this.

That meant Juice Box had his tortoise, Telly, walking around the room—he blocks all the doorways so

that Telly can't wander off and get lost. Tortoises move way faster than "The Tortoise and the Hare" would have you think. Telly has already escaped the kitchen a few times, and we've found him in the strangest places.

I have no idea how Telly climbed down twelve steps to the basement.

As I was getting some cereal, Mom and Dad walked in with Finn and Fern. They got these funny looks when they saw me, so I knew something was up.

I was surprised Mom said that, too—I thought she'd be thrilled. But then she explained.

Then Mom and Dad got in a deep conversation about men and women, and who should do what. They didn't even hear our doorbell ring. It was my friend and neighbor, Chloe, who goes to a private school across town.

Chloe looked *very* awake for seven in the morning. She was practically vibrating.

I had no idea what she was talking about.

Dreamy? I wasn't sure about *that*.

Then we heard someone call out from the street. It was Ursula, our neighbor—she was out walking one of her cats. Mr. Howdy, who runs Art Club at my school, was with her. I guess they're boyfriend-girlfriend these days.

Wait. Does *everyone* know about Manners Class?

Ursula continued.

Mom said Manners Class seemed old-fashioned, and Ursula is the least old-fashioned person I've ever met. She has a thousand animals. And there's a *cauldron* in her house.

But Ursula says that learning good manners is fun—and useful.

I guess I'll see soon enough.

THE THANK YOU NOTE

Dear Cosmo,

It was a normal morning. We had a Math Relay Race that I bombed as usual. We had a geography quiz about the Southern states—I think I got an eight out of ten on it, because I always mix up Alabama and Arkansas. Then Miss Kettle and Steve introduced a new unit in English on poetry by acting out their favorite poem, "The Raven," by Edgar Allan Poe.

I have no idea where Miss Kettle got that strange bird hat.

Finally, it was lunchtime. At twelve on the dot, Mrs. Wink arrived in our doorway to take the Manners Class lunch bunch for our very first lesson. Then we picked up the other two fifth-grade classrooms as well. There were quite a few of us following Mrs. Wink.

We proceeded down the hall, past the cafeteria, to a very surprising place.

We were having our meeting in the teachers' lounge? *Wow.* It's a big secret room where teachers go to have lunch and stuff, and no kids are usually allowed. I've heard lots of rumors about all the fun things inside.

But then Mrs. Wink opened the lounge doors. And we saw *this*.

I agreed. I was really hoping there would be VR headsets.

I sat next to Rocco at a small table; Maria and Petra sat with some other girls near us. Kristian joined Oliver and some of the boys at a long table at the back.

Then Mrs. Wink clapped her hands and said she had a few additional teachers to introduce, including the *founder* of Manners Class.

I couldn't believe who they were.

It's always weird to think of school staff having families outside of school, Cosmo. I kind of want to believe that they leave BJP Elementary and go seal themselves inside a cardboard box until the next day or something.

Also, Mrs. Wink's mother and daughter are so . . . different from her.

And I've never seen *anyone* bossing Mrs. Wink around.

Mrs. Wink's mother—er, Madame Wink—started to explain the point of Manners Class.

For a minute there, it seemed like Petra's question broke Madame Wink's brain. But then she just shook it off and kept talking.

But I guess that wasn't what Madame Wink meant, because Chelsea Wink started to pass around construction paper and markers in a rainbow of colors. I noticed a table of boys got a lot of cool green markers, including a bright neon green. A few tables got a glittery gold marker. Rocco and I got a lot of great blues and oranges and this white marker that you could use against a black background.

Anyway, then Chelsea Wink said this.

We groaned. We've all been forced to write thank you notes before.

Riley raised her hand and said what we were all thinking.

Maria loves anything having to do with the queen.

Chelsea Wink asked us to think of a few

people we'd like to thank. Our note didn't have to be a thank you for a gift or an invitation, either—it could just be a thank you for a nice meal, or for someone who helped us with homework, or for someone who gave up the tire swing on the playground at recess so we could use it instead. There was no thank you too small. We could even thank things, not just people!

So we all started to brainstorm.

We got to work. First I wrote a note to Dad thanking him for getting me through the pickleball tournament. Then I wrote a note to Mr. Howdy for encouraging me to write and draw. I wrote a note to Billy J. Plumberry thanking him for a nice weekend in New York. I wrote a note to Maria thanking her for fast-forwarding through the scary parts of horror movies when we have sleepovers. I didn't have enough time, but I will definitely write notes to the rest of my friends as well—and to Mom, Juice Box, Grandma Mimi... and I guess Grandma Anne, too, for letting me take care of Bobert the puppy while she was away.

I have to say, it was nice to thank people and make them feel special, and I kept thinking of more people to add to my list of notes. We all chatted about more people we might send thank you notes to. Even Chelsea Wink, who had a *very* long list. We learned a few interesting things about her.

And Kristian says nothing dangerous happens on carnival rides!

At the end of the lunch period, the Winks said that if we'd written a note to someone here today, we could pass it to them now. So I handed my notes around, and when I got back to my seat, I saw a pile of notes people had written to me, too. To my delight, I got a note from Maria! And Violet! And Steve the hippo!

At the bottom of my pile was another note, but it wasn't signed. It was written with the cool neon-green marker that I'd noticed at the table where most of the boys sat.

Then I read the note. And everything sort of . . . changed.

You are pretty?
What does *that* mean?

CRUSHES

Dear Cosmo,

I stuffed the mysterious anonymous thank you note in my backpack and zipped the pocket tight. I didn't want anyone to see it. I felt sort of . . . *embarrassed* by it.

My head was spinning. Someone thought I was . . . pretty? Was that just a compliment, or did that mean someone . . . *liked* me? A boy wrote the note, for sure—I knew because of that neon-green pen. I even checked the markers at all the other tables just to be sure, but that neon marker was *only* at the table where all those boys sat.

Did boys usually go around saying girls were pretty? I kind of had a feeling they didn't. So . . . now what? Am I supposed to respond? If I ask the Winks, they'll probably tell me I should send a thank you note for the thank you note. But . . . how can I write back if I don't even know who wrote it?

And what will I *say*?

What a disaster. What if I say the wrong thing? What if I make the note writer upset? What if I give the wrong message? Why is someone saying this to me at all?

The rest of the day passed in a blur. I barely remember walking home, but Chloe was waiting for me on my front porch. She leapt up as soon as she saw me, excited to know what happened in Manners Class. So I told her about the Winks, eating in the teachers' lounge, and how we had to write thank you notes to each other.

Then Chloe asked something surprising.

Wait. Boys? Who cared about boys?

This was all news to me.

What was Chloe *talking* about?

Something suddenly occurred to me that made my stomach flip. Maybe crushes *were* the new thing at my school after all.

Chloe must have seen the uncomfortable look on my face, because she asked me what was wrong. And I couldn't help it, Cosmo. I just blurted it out.

But I wasn't so sure it was amazing.
I wasn't so sure about *anything*.

PENNY HAIKU

Dear Cosmo,

I tossed and turned all night, thinking non-stop about crushes. Chloe suddenly had crushes. Apparently, so did her whole class. And now—maybe—someone from my class had a crush on *me*.

When had this happened? *Did* everyone in fifth grade have crushes now? How had I missed this? Maybe there was some sort of memo that went around the fifth grade recently, and I was the only one who didn't receive it.

FIFTH-GRADE MEMO:
To: All Fifth Graders (except Penny)
Subject: We all have crushes now!

But I tried to hide my jitters when I went down to breakfast. There was no way Mom could know about any of this. She would blow it way out of proportion.

But as it turned out, I didn't have to hide anything. When I went downstairs, Mom wasn't anywhere. And *this* was happening.

Juice Box burst into tears. I haven't seen him cry so hard since we went to Monster Jam last year and one of his favorite trucks caught on fire and couldn't take part in the wheelie competition.

Dad, who hadn't left for work yet, asked him to slow down and explain. He couldn't even speak for a few minutes. His legs were wobbling so badly.

Dad reassured Juice Box that it was very unlikely that Telly was outside. We always kept the doors closed to keep *you* in, Cosmo, and it was pretty unlikely Telly knew how to use a doorknob. Surely he was just hiding somewhere, like always.

So we started to look for him.

We looked on the first floor and the second floor. We even looked in the babies' room, which was tricky, because Mom had just gotten Finn and Fern down for their morning naps. We had to be very quiet.

But Telly wasn't anywhere. Not the basement. Not the random powder room on the first floor no one uses.

Juice Box got more and more upset.

Juice Box had preschool today, but Mom let him stay home just this once so they could look for Telly. I really didn't want to leave Juice Box to go to *my* school, but I had no choice. I kind of wished I had stayed home, though, because when I got to the school steps, I overheard Riley, Lulu, and Violet talking together.

And wouldn't you know, they were talking about crushes.

I wasn't surprised that Riley and Lulu have crushes. But *Violet*? During one of our last sleepovers in June, Violet said *this*.

I heard someone calling my name. Maria, Rocco, Petra, and Kristian were waving me over from the other side of the stairs. When I got closer, Kristian frowned at me.

I *was* stressed. I wanted to tell my friends about the anonymous thank you note, but then the bell rang, and we all had to go inside. Which was maybe for the best, to be honest. I felt so embarrassed about all of it. I had no idea what I would even say.

In my classroom, Miss Kettle and Steve were ready to start the English unit about poetry.

I tried to listen, but my mind wandered. I kept looking around the room at the boys. Normally, I think of the boys in terms of "that kid who hums a lot" or "that kid who won the Geography Bee" or "that kid who's really good at making strawberry milk come out of his nose when he laughs."

But now when I looked at the boys, I thought this.

Miss Kettle said it was time to write a haiku of our own, making the first line five syllables, the second line seven syllables, and the last line five syllables again. I tried to write about poetic topics like cherry blossoms, or summer rain, or the way your paws smell like Fritos, Cosmo.

But all my haikus ended up being about one thing only.

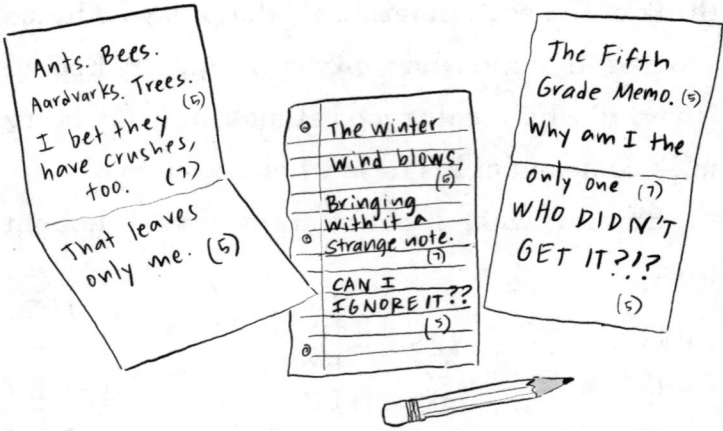

Miss Kettle and Steve walked around looking at everyone's poems. And, well, I guess Miss Kettle was a little concerned about mine.

So that's exactly what I did.

THE BOAT

Dear Cosmo,

A few minutes later, I was sitting in Mrs. Hines's office. Technically, she was on a break between students, but she said she could squeeze me in for a few minutes as long as I didn't mind if she drank a cup of tea while we talked.

Mrs. Hines asked what had given me *that* idea.

I wasn't sure whether I should believe her. Sometimes kids know more about these things than adults.

Then I told her about the anonymous note I'd received that said I was pretty.

Hmm. I didn't know what to think about that.

"We have to look out for our *own* feelings, too," Mrs. Hines added.

Then she circled back to my worry that everyone had crushes except for me. I told her how Chloe announced that she liked boys and that she bet lots of kids in my class had crushes, too. Then I told her how I overheard some other girls, including Violet, gossiping about how *they* had crushes, so maybe it was true. What if everyone in my class—including my friends—was starting to have crushes on people? What if I was the only one who *didn't*? What if people would think I was a baby if I admitted that? I just wasn't ready for all this crush stuff! Why did things have to change? Why couldn't they stay the same?

Mrs. Hines argued that things weren't changing as fast as I thought.

I wanted to think she wasn't just saying all of this to make me feel better. Maybe there were some kids in my class who felt the same way I did, *terrified* about the idea of liking people or things like that. But at the moment, the boat I was in seemed more like a little rowboat than a megayacht. Leaky, unsteady, and only big enough for me.

SLURPING UP THE CLUES

Dear Cosmo,

The last few days have been stressful. First of all, Telly is still lost. We've tried everything to find him. Juice Box put out all of Telly's favorite treats—edible flowers, nonprickly cactus pads, big crispy leaves of lettuce—in hopes that maybe he'll come out to nibble on them. Then he set up an old phone next to the traps and downloaded a motion recording app. He was sure the camera would catch Telly waddling into the frame.

But then he watched the playback.

Dad had a good outlook, though.

Mom took Dad into another room and started whispering about something. I tried to listen in, but I couldn't tell what they were saying. Great. Did I have to worry about them keeping another secret? I mean, it can't be that they're having more babies. They already seem overwhelmed with the twins.

There are more things to worry about, too. The suspense is killing me about who wrote my secret admirer note . . . but I'm not sure who to talk to or where to turn. I mean, I'm still so embarrassed about the note, I haven't even taken it out of my backpack yet!

So far, I've only told Henry. Sort of.

Yesterday, when I came home from school, Chloe was waiting for me on the sidewalk, and she was jiggling with excitement.

She meant my secret admirer, of course. There was part of me that wished I hadn't blurted out all that stuff about the note, but, well . . . the cat is already out of the bag.

Which is a really weird expression, by the way.

Anyway, I tried to change the subject.

When Chloe gets something in her head, it's hard to talk her out of it. And I *am* curious about who wrote that note. So I said fine, we could try to solve the mystery.

Chloe ran back into her house, saying she had to "set the mystery-solving mood" with a certain costume from her big costume stash. She reappeared looking like this.

But then Chloe realized she couldn't really move in the milkshake costume, so she ran back into her house and changed again.

But Chloe insisted. She got a big notepad and a pencil to start.

We wrote down the names of the boys who sat at that table in Manners Class. The problem was that there were so many—it was one of those long tables that seats tons of people. In fact, the only boy I knew who *hadn't* sat there was Rocco, because he'd sat with me.

Chloe asked if maybe the handwriting could give something away. She wanted to see it ... but I said that I'd rather keep it to myself. I was still so embarrassed.

Before Chloe left, she gave me some advice.

And so, today, that's exactly what I've been doing. And I thought for a moment I had a break in the case. During recess, Oliver Bracca came over to my friends and me on the blacktop.

Was Oliver joking? Everyone knew that pickleball was *not* my favorite activity. I nearly quit the team!

But Oliver seemed serious. And it seemed like he was asking only *me*, not anyone else in the group. Like maybe he wanted to get me alone or something.

And then I realized: Oliver had been sitting at that long table during Manners Class! Maybe he'd used that green pen. I couldn't remember what his handwriting was like, but what if it was very neat?

Could Oliver have written that note? Did he think I was pretty?

I wasn't ready to handle talking to my secret admirer face-to-face, but I also didn't want to be rude and tell Oliver that I didn't want to play, either. Luckily, Kristian stepped in.

Rocco said he'd like to play as well. Rocco and Kristian beat us easily, both because they're pretty good at pickleball and because I was extremely distracted the whole time, searching for more clues that Oliver was my secret admirer. Not that I found anything out.

But then, at the end of the game, we all started talking.

Aha! If Oliver only wrote *one* thank you letter during Manners Class, and that thank you note was to Mr. Lamb . . . that meant he *couldn't* have written the one to me that said I was pretty. And so I could eliminate him from my investigation.

It made me relieved . . . but totally exhausted. This mystery-solving stuff was hard work. And also, there were tons of other boys I still needed to cross off the list.

THE TRIANGLE

Dear Cosmo,

This morning, Juice Box got up extra early to look for Telly. He emptied all the low, dusty kitchen cabinets, cleared out a large pile of dog toys, and even took apart the heating vent to see if Telly had climbed inside. But all we found were old macaroni noodles, some bones you'd forgotten about, Cosmo, and a lot of dust.

Juice Box said he was going to post the signs on all the poles outside our house *and* at his preschool, just in case Telly had stowed away in Juice Box's backpack.

...

At lunch, we were scheduled for another Manners Class. As we lined up, I kept looking around at everyone. It was weird to think that someone in this line had written that note to me.

When we got to the teachers' lounge and sat down, Madame Wink announced our next lesson.

We all groaned—politely, of course. Most of our parents had been trying to teach us table manners for years. According to them, we all eat like cavepeople.

Mrs. Wink gave everyone plates and utensils and told us how to set them out for a meal. Then Chelsea had us take out our lunches and arrange them on the plates. Madame Wink placed a basket of bread in the middle of each table and filled up some cups of water. She seemed to be annoyed that they were plastic and not something fancier, like crystal.

Then, when all that was done, she did this.

Silver chime? It looked like a plain old triangle from music class to me.

Madame Wink told us to sit down and start eating our lunches normally. So we did. But then this started happening.

I never knew a triangle could be so scary.

Every bite someone took, there Madame Wink was with that triangle, telling us we were doing it wrong. It was just *eating*. Who knew it was so complicated?

Chelsea Wink started to look really stressed.

Chelsea Wink also told us that our napkins were named Matilda—and Matildas felt most safe on our laps—and that our chairs were named Bertram, and Bertrams liked to be sat on *properly*, with no bouncing or fidgeting and definitely no tipping backward.

Madame Wink looked like her head was going to explode.

Then Petra raised her hand and said something that *really* pushed Madame Wink over the edge.

Madame Wink stared at Petra for a long time. I'm not sure she blinked. All of us were too afraid to giggle, even though Petra was kind of right.

Then Mrs. Wink stepped in. I hoped that she'd save the day in a Goldilocks way. Like, if Madame Wink was the Wink that was too hard, and Chelsea Wink was the Wink that was too soft, then maybe Mrs. Wink would be the Wink that was just right.

Except then she said this.

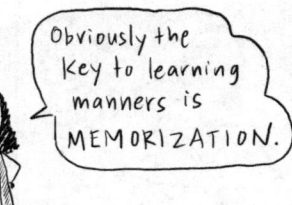

Mrs. Wink wheeled over this huge whiteboard that listed all of the rules about table manners. Some of them were in such tiny writing, we had to squint to read it.

Then she made us take notes.

As we were all feverishly scribbling, I felt a tap on my arm. It was Michael McMinnamin, who was sitting at the table next to mine. He held out an oversized pencil for me.

I took it and said thank you, because Madame Wink was watching and I didn't want to be rude . . . but I was confused. Why did Michael want to give *me* his museum pencil?

Suddenly, I felt very strange. Could *Michael* be my secret admirer? He'd been sitting at that table of boys the other day when we wrote those thank you notes. He could have used that green pen.

This was awkward. Michael was nice and everything, and we'd sort of had a special moment when I loaned him my magic paddle during the pickleball tournament . . . but *Riley* liked him. She'd liked him since kindergarten!

I must have been kind of wriggling in my seat, because Maria noticed.

Maria whispered that maybe I should stop fidgeting—otherwise Madame Wink might come around with her triangle again or Chelsea Wink would say I'd hurt Bertram the chair's feelings.

I glanced one last time in Michael's direction, and that's when I noticed his paper with all his notes. And ... hmm. I'd never really looked at his handwriting before.

Or, well, I *think* it was handwriting.

My secret admirer's handwriting is very neat. So I guess Michael is off the list, too.

Phew.

THE LANGUAGE OF T

Dear Cosmo,

After school, Kristian ran up to me. I had told him about Telly going missing, and he had a plan.

Kristian said he was certain he could talk to Telly in this secret language to coax him out of his hiding place. I figured we could give it a try. Juice Box was desperate.

I asked Maria if she wanted to come, too, but she wasn't so sure.

She was really taking Manners Class to heart.

I asked Petra next, but Petra looked kind of embarrassed.

Whoa. That seemed harsh.

But Petra wasn't that worried. Turns out, a few kids had gotten special permission to do a project in the library instead of manners, and Petra figured her mom would probably be fine if she did that, too.

Petra said she wanted to go home and talk to her mom to smooth things over, so Kristian and I headed to my house on our own. The whole way there, Kristian talked about his favorite topic: roller coasters. I wanted to listen, but I just couldn't stop thinking about how I hadn't gotten any closer to figuring out who my secret admirer was.

When we got home, Kristian marched right over to Juice Box, who was already searching for Telly again around the couch.

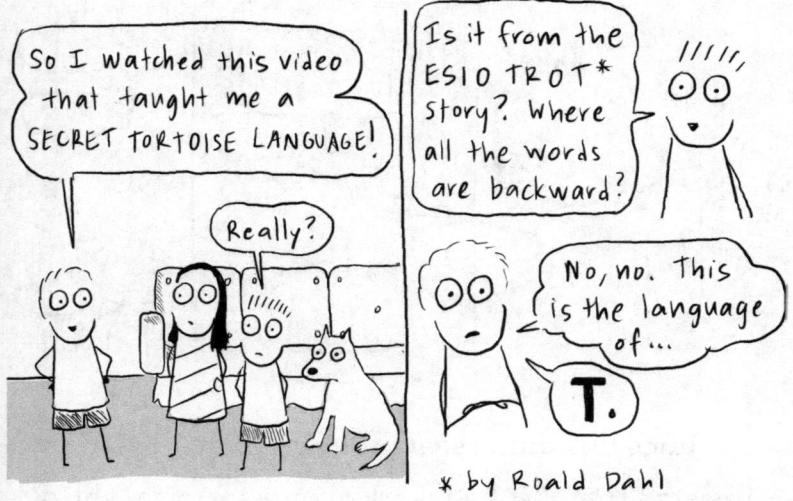

*by Roald Dahl

I'd never heard of the language of T, but Kristian had seen a demonstration in a YouTube video. He showed it to us. I have to say, it was pretty interesting. Apparently, tortoises really understand the *t* sound. When you make the *t* sound—gently, with your eyes closed—they come out from where they're hiding. It's like snake charming, sort of. One video told the story of this guy who found a tortoise who'd been hiding for *seventy-five years*—and he did it just by calling out to him in the language of T.

Kristian went first.

Juice Box didn't seem convinced, but Kristian insisted that if it had worked on a tortoise who'd been hiding for seventy-five years, it would work for Telly. So we all tried. The problem was, the language of T only worked if you did it with your eyes closed. Kristian said it had something to do with tortoises feeling more comfortable revealing themselves if you didn't see where their hiding spots were.

When Juice Box went flying over that truck, Mom said that whatever we were doing, we needed to stop.

But Kristian wasn't discouraged.

I hoped so.

THE GALA

Dear Cosmo,

If I told you that Chloe has sent me at least a hundred more texts wanting to know if I've gotten any closer to figuring out who my secret admirer is, I don't think I'd be lying.

But actually, I have ruled out two more boys. First off, there's Anders, who's in Ms. Letts's class. I figured out that he isn't my secret admirer because he came to school with cupcakes for this girl named Bettina.

Then there's Colin, who sits behind Riley in Miss Kettle's class.

Everyone knows boys only put boogers on your desk if they like you. Not that I understand that at *all*. Boys are so strange. But I guess it isn't him, either.

This morning, as all of us were waiting on the steps for the bell to ring, Petra had exciting news. You know how I said that people who were skipping manners had to do a special project instead? Well, Petra had come up with what her special project was going to be.

We all started gobbling like turkeys to try it out.

Then Petra said something else about her new manners system.

Oh yeah. We were having a party at the end of Manners Class—I'd kind of forgotten about it because of all the secret admirer stuff.

Petra thanked Maria for the offer, but she was afraid that there would be too many traditional manners required at a restaurant. Ideally, her party should be somewhere like an open field, where there were no limits or rooms or walls.

Maria also had news. She said that since she's really gotten into all this manners stuff, she's now taking an online course that will teach her even *more* manners on top of the manners we're already learning with the Winks.

But Maria insisted they aren't chores—it's all about *hospitality*. Making people feel welcome and comfortable when they're in your home. It still sounds like chores to me, though.

I was afraid Petra was going to say something about how proper and stuffy that all seemed, but instead she just smiled calmly.

I think I like the Way of Petra.

We settled down in our homerooms, but before we could even say the pledge, the PA system crackled. Madame Wink's elegant voice came through the speakers.

Yes, Cosmo, at that moment, it really seemed like Madame Wink was speaking in cursive letters.

Miss Kettle grumbled about this pop-up assembly because Madame Wink was interrupting her lesson on poems, but she dismissed everyone in Manners Class to go see what she wanted.

We filed into the multipurpose room. When we got there, all three Winks were standing on the stage, wearing fancy clothes.

Well, Chelsea and Madame Wink had on fancy clothes. Mrs. Wink still had on her crossing guard outfit, though I did notice she'd bedazzled her stop sign.

Madame Wink stepped forward and started to speak.

She pronounced gala like *gah-lah*. First off, she said, she would like to remind us that we must dress *appropriately* for this party. All three Winks described the dress code.

Then Madame Wink told us about something else that would be happening at the party.

Dances? As in... we're going to have to dance? Like... *with other people*? Like... *crushes*?

As I looked around, *everyone* was talking excitedly.

But I didn't feel excited at all. Dancing sounded intimidating. And it seemed like I was the only girl *not* excited to dance with someone. I don't know what Mrs. Hines was talking about when she said that lots of kids in my grade didn't care about crushes. Because from where I sat, I was definitely the only one in the no-crushes boat.

And now *this* was happening.

FANCY PANTS

Dear Cosmo,

Not only is the big Manners Party the teenager kind, but it's also turned into a gala where we have to wear fancy clothes *and* do fancy dances. What's next? Are we all going to have to speak in British accents, too?

Actually, that might be kind of fun.

There was part of me that wished that I, like Petra, had also chosen to do a special project instead of manners. At the same time, I didn't want to abandon my friends. Especially when I noticed, at the end of the school day, that Rocco looked sort of nervous. He was concerned about this new wrinkle in the Manners Party, too.

I told Rocco that I was sure he'd be good at dancing if he practiced. He was good at anything he put his mind to—like pickleball and art—and he was a great leader on the New York trip.

But Rocco was pretty certain dancing was different.

The clarinet player—who just happened to be passing by on his way to an after-school band rehearsal—started playing a tune. And, well, this happened.

It was like Rocco's feet had been abducted by aliens.

I wasn't sure how to help him with dancing, since I don't really know how to dance, either, but I did tell him I could go shopping this afternoon to pick out some new clothes. After Rocco called his dad for a ride and I texted my mom to see if I could go, I called Chloe to see if she could join, too, because Chloe *loves* to dress people up.

Petra walked up just then, and we asked her if she wanted to come shopping with us, too. But Petra didn't seem very interested in fancy clothes.

When we all met up at the mall, Chloe whispered the same question she'd been asking me for days.

I whispered back to Chloe that, *no*, I hadn't figured out who my secret admirer was since the *last* time she asked, which was twelve minutes ago.

We headed through the mall entrance. Inside, the air smelled like pretzels from the pretzel cart. Kids were shrieking at the indoor playground. High school students were trying out phones and gadgets at the high-tech store. This was one of the first times I'd ever been to the mall alone with friends, Cosmo. I felt sort of . . . *grown-up*.

Chloe marched us straight to a clothes store. And once we got there, she knew just what to do.

Rocco wasn't so sure about *that*.

Too late. The saleswoman ran to the back to find Rocco's size. A few minutes later, she came out with all kinds of pants that were *quite* fancy. One pair had a lot of zippers. Another was made of blue leather. And another pair was kind of . . . confusing.

Chloe was very excited about the idea of fancy silkworms, but Rocco put his foot down. He could barely walk in the pants, they were so long. He also said they itched, like maybe some of the silkworms were still *living* in the pants. He used the money his dad gave him on some regular black pants that were very nice and didn't itch.

Then Chloe got excited about accessories.

Rocco said he'd only consider the top hat. Not the cane, and definitely not a monocle—not that the store even *sold* one of those.

I was giggling at all of this, but suddenly, things turned kind of . . . weird. As Rocco tried the hat on, Chloe said something totally surprising.

Chloe glanced at Rocco—she said Maria had told her something while they were studying for another upcoming Spelling Bee yesterday. Rocco's cheeks flushed. His voice kind of cracked when he said what he said next.

Maria loves this show called *The Great Icelandic Cake-Off*, a competitive baking show set in Iceland. I've watched it with Maria a few times, and it's sort of entertaining . . . but also sort of weird. Maria is always swooning for this one guy named Sven. He does all of his baking while sitting on an Icelandic horse.

The horse gets a little annoyed when Sven has to use the giant mixer or the waffle iron.

But to be honest, Cosmo, I felt a little shocked that Maria and Rocco were going to the Manners Party together. I mean, it's totally fine for *them*. Maria and Rocco are friends. But . . . does that mean that *lots* of people are going to go together?

And—oh no. Does this mean my secret admirer is going to ask *me*?

EXTREME BED MAKING

Dear Cosmo,

It's Tuesday. Four days until the Manners Party. I'm really ramping up trying to figure out who my secret admirer is. I've ruled out a couple more people.

But it hasn't gotten me much closer to solving the mystery. My secret admirer is out there, and I feel like they're going to reveal themselves soon, especially if people are asking other people to the Manners Party as dates. I've already heard that Riley is going with Michael McMinnamin—of course—and Lulu is going with Oliver, and Mr. Howdy is bringing Ursula as an extra chaperone.

It's made me very jumpy, I have to say. Every time a boy even looks at me, I'm afraid they're going to ambush me with the question.

Luckily, it was only Maria tapping me on the shoulder. She'd come up to me on the sidewalk after school let out.

I'd forgotten to make my bed that morning, so actually, Maria would be helping me out. I was excited to hang out with her anyway. She has been so busy studying manners and I've been so busy panicking about all this secret admirer stuff that I've hardly seen her.

I still feel unsure about sharing all of that with Maria. The thing is, it's been more than a week since I got the note, and now it feels sort of weird to say something. Maria might wonder why I didn't tell her sooner.

We got to my house and headed up to my room. On the way, though, I saw Juice Box doing this.

Neither of us knew what to say. I can't imagine if *you* went missing, Cosmo. I'd feel devastated.

Maria and I went into my room so she could practice her bed making. Maria told me to rip the covers off. Then she asked me to time her on how quickly she could make my bed again.

I'd barely started the timer app on my phone when she started flicking my comforter through the air.

She was done so quickly, and the bed looked . . . well, way better than when *I* made my bed.

Then Maria asked me this.

Too *slow*?

Maria took all of my sheets and pillows and the comforter off the bed and started over again. As she smoothed the sheet over the mattress, I mentioned how Rocco told me that he and Maria were going to the Manners Party together. She explained why she'd asked him.

Then I asked her this, as casually as I could.

Not a big deal? Maria and I definitely didn't live on the same planet, because to me it was a huge, *stressful* deal!

Then, Maria looked up at me like I'd said that out loud.

I could feel you looking at me, Cosmo. It was like you wanted me to tell Maria what's been going on. She's so kind and nice. Maybe she would help with things, just like she's helping Rocco.

I still felt so embarrassed, though. Was it weird to have a secret admirer? Would it seem like I was bragging? I really, *really* wished I'd never gotten that note. I felt envious of Maria, too. She got to go with Rocco, a friend. That seemed like so much fun.

But that gave me an idea. Could I ask someone else to the Manners Party? A *friend*? That way, even if my secret admirer did ask me, I could say that, sorry, I was already going with someone else. I wouldn't have to hurt anyone's feelings by saying I didn't like them back.

I looked at Maria and smiled.

SOME ANSWERS

Dear Cosmo,

It was Wednesday morning. Three days until the Manners Party. But I wasn't worried anymore. I had a plan. I was going to ask a friend to go with me. I was going to ask ... Kristian!

It was such a relief.

I set off to school early. I was hoping to ask Kristian on the steps before school started, but he wasn't there.

Then I tried to catch Kristian in the hall as his class went to art and our class went to music, but he was deep in a conversation with Luke about something very important.

Then it was lunchtime. We didn't have manners today, so we sat down at our normal table in the cafeteria.

Kristian got up to stand in the soft pretzel line. The line always takes forever because the pretzels sell out fast and the lunch staff has to bake the new pretzels from scratch. Today, the line was *extra long*, so it took until the end of lunch for Kristian to return to our table, pretzel in hand.

I took a piece as we lined up to head back to class. Then I breathed in, ready to ask. Here was my chance. I don't know why I was so nervous. It was just the Manners Party, and we were just friends.

But then a voice interrupted me. Miss Kettle, along with the other two fifth-grade teachers, stood in the hallway hanging up the poems we'd written for the poetry unit.

Kristian and I turned to check out the poems. None of the ones I'd written were up there, thankfully—they all had to do with worries about crushes and boys and the Manners Party. I'm glad Miss Kettle realized that I'd be embarrassed to let anyone else read them.

But then I noticed something about one of the poems. Something . . . *shocking*.

There was something awfully . . . *familiar* about one poem's handwriting. It was so neat. Orderly. Exactly like the handwriting on a certain thank you note.

My stomach sank to my knees. I'd just figured out who my secret admirer was.

Kristian.

GUMBALL MACHINE RING

Dear Cosmo,

My head was spinning. *Kristian* wrote me that note? *Kristian* thought I was pretty? Kristian . . . *liked me?*

I hadn't even *considered* him. He's my friend! Practically my *best* friend! I thought I'd be able to sense it if he felt that way . . . but I had no idea! And wait, is that why he came over to my house to help find Telly? Is that why he offered to play pickleball with me against Oliver?

Or . . . was he just being friendly? Like always?

I felt so confused. And worse, all this had occurred to me in the middle of the hallway . . . *with Kristian standing right next to me.*

I couldn't actually ask him to the Manners Party *now*. If I said that I wanted to go with him, he'd think I liked him, too, wouldn't he? And *then* what would happen?

I ran into the bathroom to get away. I couldn't believe this. I'd spent all of this time trying to not be caught off guard by my secret admirer's identity, and I'd never felt so surprised in my life. But I also felt terrible. This was Kristian! I couldn't lose him as a friend! Should I just say I liked him? Maybe it would make him so happy. Maybe it was fine if it wasn't the truth. But . . . maybe he'd be able to tell that I didn't actually like him for real. I didn't like *anyone*. He'd probably hate me.

This was a disaster.

...

Finally, when I was sure everyone had returned to their classrooms after lunch, I snuck back into my class and fell into my seat. Miss Kettle and Steve introduced the latest poem we would be writing: the sonnet. Apparently, it's a poem often about love. *Perfect.*

The last thing I wanted to think about right now was writing a love poem. I was trying to get *away* from love! And my mind was still churning. I kept trying to retrace my steps. When had Kristian developed a crush on me? Had it been during pickleball practice? Had it been when we were in New York City? Or maybe the treasure hunt when we went to Adventure Land? And—oh *no*. Had he told all my friends about this? Did they all know?

Around me, everyone else was scratching away, writing their sonnets. But I raised my hand for Miss Kettle.

I felt like I wasn't making any sense, but I guess Miss Kettle got the picture. She gave me a hall pass, and I ran down to Mrs. Hines's office.

But to my surprise, I saw *this* on the door.

Was this some kind of *answering service*? Where the heck *was* she? Then our principal, Mr. Mortion, came down the hall and noticed me standing there.

Oh yes. Sometimes Mrs. Hines goes into the classrooms and does feelings lessons with all of us. It's great that she does that, but *I* needed her. And there was no way I was writing my problem on one of the little sticky notes and leaving it in that basketball hoop for the whole school to see. That would be humiliating.

Mr. Mortion told me to go back to class and headed down the hall. Unfortunately, that meant I had the whole afternoon to get through. Somehow I made it, pretty much avoiding Kristian—and my other friends—the whole time.

When the bell rang, I ran out to the curb to walk home. But then I saw someone familiar.

I'd forgotten that Grandma Mimi was my ride today. Sometimes she picks me up for what she calls "Grandma Mimi Adventures." It's special Penny and Mimi bonding time, and we've done lots of fun stuff.

It was really fun watching those horses run, I have to say.

The thing was, I didn't think I could fake happiness for a Grandma Mimi Adventure. I suddenly had to get my troubles off my chest. So there, next to the bus loading zone, I just blurted it out.

Grandma Mimi took off her glasses, rubbed them with the end of her shirt, and then put them back on again. It's something she always does when she's thinking hard.

Grandma Mimi and I walked to her car. I had no idea where we were going to go, but she said not to worry about it. First, we went to a fast-food drive-thru and got some milkshakes. Then we drove to this sculpture garden Grandma Mimi said she and her Grandma Group toured recently. It was a nice day for a walk, she said, and the outdoor sculptures were . . . *interesting*.

We walked around for a while. We drank our milkshakes. I kind of thought Grandma Mimi had forgotten all about my question about crushes. But then she said this.

Grandma Mimi sighed.

No, no, Grandma Mimi said. He just wanted to go to the school carnival together. Also, it wasn't a real diamond ring. It was out of a gumball machine.

But this was similar to my problem, actually. Just like Nate Quigley put a gumball machine ring in Grandma Mimi's mailbox as an invitation to the carnival, Kristian had written me a note and probably wanted to go to the Manners Party together. Maybe I could learn from her experience.

Grandma Mimi sighed. She said, actually, that she *didn't*. Not exactly.

Grandma Mimi started saying something else, something more about how she would have done things differently if she could do it over again, but my mind was already a million miles away. Grandma Mimi had politely avoided Nate Quigley, and he didn't bother her about his crush again. Could that work with Kristian? I mean, there were only a few more days until the Manners Party. Could I just . . . *politely* avoid Kristian until then? I'd use really nice manners, of course. And then maybe Kristian would get the hint somehow. Maybe he'd even forget about his crush on me, and we would stay friends, and everything would go back to normal.

Then Grandma Mimi looked at me carefully.

I didn't see the point in telling Grandma Mimi about Kristian and the note anymore, since I already had my solution.

I was so relieved that I threw my arms around Grandma Mimi. She seemed sort of surprised, but she's always down for a hug.

CHITCHAT

Dear Cosmo,

Well, Operation Polite Avoidance is underway. Though, I have to say, it's hard to avoid Kristian and make it look natural. For example, he sent me a few texts last night. Whenever one came in, I was terrified it was going to be about the secret admirer note or the Manners Party, but they were all just new ideas to track down Telly. He even sent Juice Box a special package.

Juice Box sprinkled the Tortoise Nip around right away—well, after we made sure it wasn't harmful to dogs, that is. We knew you'd want to sample some, Cosmo.

But Telly hasn't come out yet.

I politely texted Kristian back, thanking him for the Tortoise Nip, but that was all. Like Mimi had done with Nate Quigley and the school carnival, I was going to make sure Kristian and I didn't interact very much before the Manners Party. And then maybe this would all just . . . go away.

I hoped so, anyway.

This morning, I knew I couldn't show up to school early because all of my friends, including Kristian, hang out on the steps before the bell rings. Going to school late *really* isn't my thing, and it felt weird to dillydally on my walk, but by the time I got there, nearly everyone had gone inside.

Except Petra. She was late, too. And she looked troubled.

Then she looked at me.

I'm all for the Way of Petra, but it sounds like the party might be messy and chaotic. Mom has been pretty stressed out with taking care of the babies *and* looking for Telly. I'm not sure she'll let me have a party anytime soon.

I told Petra I'd ask but I couldn't make any promises.

The morning went by in a blur, and soon enough, we were lining up for our last Manners Class before the big party—or *gala*, as Madame Wink called it. I made sure to stay away from Kristian in the line. That was sort of complicated, because it meant I had to stay away from *all* of my friends.

I mumbled something about having a pebble stuck in my shoe and that they should go ahead without me.

Today, Madame Wink was taking us somewhere special.

I wasn't even sure what high tea *was*, but apparently it took place outside of school property. Our parents had even had to sign permission slips.

Madame Wink also roped Miss Kettle, Ms. Letts, and Mr. Glenn into coming along as chaperones. The fifth-grade teachers didn't look particularly thrilled to be missing their lunch break... but, well, Madame Wink can be kind of convincing. Even Steve didn't want to cross her.

Madame Wink led us out the side door and down the street. And even though I was trying to keep my distance from Kristian—which meant, unfortunately, the rest of my friends, too—I did overhear Rocco saying this.

Also on the walk, Chelsea Wink had an . . . incident.

Madame Wink finally stopped in front of the place where we'd have our "high tea."

Everyone cheered. We all love O's Diner. They have the best pancakes in town. I'm not really sure they have high tea, whatever that even is, but Madame Wink didn't seem to care.

Because Madame Wink had a plan.

Social skills? Don't we know those already?

I mean, isn't that just talking to people? Mrs. Hines gives us lessons about that all the time.

But Madame Wink said social skills were an *art*. She explained more as we walked into the diner.

To demonstrate, Madame Wink asked Chelsea to introduce herself. She said she would start with several *impolite* versions of meeting and greeting someone—things we *shouldn't* do.

We all giggled. We'd never seen Madame Wink be so rude. But it seemed quite obvious. I mean, who would tell someone her hair looked weird?

Madame Wink seemed to think she was teaching us something truly groundbreaking.

Riley said what we all were thinking ... but I'm not sure she realized how *loudly* she said it. Madame Wink stopped her lesson, got this angry look on her face, and hurried over to Riley.

Madame Wink said that we would practice introducing ourselves, making eye contact, and engaging in what she called "chitchat," polite conversation one might have at high tea.

Mrs. Wink stepped in to talk more about chitchat.

It was *very* strange hearing those words coming out of an adult's mouth. And it looked like Madame Wink might explode.

Finally, the server tapped Madame Wink's shoulder.

The server showed us to a bunch of booths, and everyone started to pile in. Maria and Rocco slid into one side of one, and Kristian slid into another. Obviously, in normal times, I'd join them... but today I froze.

I couldn't sit there and make chitchat. I had to come up with another plan. Fast.

My friends looked at me like I wasn't making any sense, but I ran to another booth and fell into a seat.

When I looked around at the people at the table, I felt a little . . . unsure.

Okay, so I do know those kids, just not that well. But maybe it's a good thing to connect with people I don't know.

We ordered, and some food and cups of peppermint tea (of course) came out fast. While we ate, Madame Wink went around critiquing our manners. She wasn't allowed to use the triangle at the diner, so she just snapped her fingers.

I twisted around to see who Madame Wink was talking about. Turns out, it was Kristian. He was just sort of . . . staring.

I bit my lip. Kristian looked so sad. Was it because I was sitting at a different table? I'd been trying to spare his feelings by politely avoiding him, but maybe I'd made things worse.

Suddenly, I didn't feel so polite at all.

NOSY RILEY

Dear Cosmo,

After tea, we headed back to school so we could go to the playground for recess. I took my place in line with the kids from the other booth, and I kept an eye on Kristian ahead of me. I tried to tell myself that maybe he looked upset for a reason that had nothing to do with me sitting somewhere else. I mean, maybe he just found out that they were tearing down one of his favorite roller coasters or something. People sit with other people all the time, right?

But I guess my behavior was more noticeable than I thought, because just as we got to the playground, Riley came up to me with a weird look on her face.

I tried to ignore her, but Riley wouldn't quit.

Riley was looking at me so intensely. I had no idea how she could tell so much or why she even cared... but that's Riley for you.

To make matters worse, when I turned around, I saw who was behind me.

Petra had found Rocco and Maria because it was recess time. I had no idea where Kristian had gone. But by the looks on their faces, they'd heard what Riley said.

And they had thoughts as well.

My friends looked at me sweetly, not in a nosy way like Riley had. They seemed genuinely worried that I had a serious problem. They *would* help me. I was sure of it. They wouldn't tease me. The problem was that my secret was about our *fifth* friend: Kristian. I didn't want to put them in the middle of things. I didn't want them to think differently of Kristian, either. But if I said nothing, they'd be hurt that I couldn't confide in them. What if they were worried that my secret was about not being friends with them anymore?

So I tried to fake my way out of it.

Then I did this weird laugh that sounded more like a nervous horse's neigh. My friends looked like they didn't really believe me, but at least they didn't ask any more questions. The problem was, though, that no one knew what to say at *all*.

Which led to this.

It seemed like hours later, but finally the bell rang that signaled the end of recess. I was actually *relieved* to go back into school.

I guess there's a first time for everything.

CONFESSIONS

Dear Cosmo,

I avoided my friends the rest of the day. Finally, it was time to go home. To my relief, Chloe wasn't waiting for me on my porch. I needed to be alone to think.

I didn't know what to do. Everything felt like a mess. I worried my friends were upset I was keeping something from them. Kristian was probably crushed because I didn't want to sit with him at the diner. I bet he guessed I didn't have a crush on him by now.

As I walked up the stairs, I pulled Kristian's thank you note out of my backpack, where I'd hidden it after Manners Class a week ago. It made me sad to look at it suddenly. What if this thank you note was the last thing Kristian ever wrote to me? What if we weren't going to be friends anymore?

As I was on the stairs, Mom called my name.

My heart sank. I bet Grandma Mimi told her about our discussion in the sculpture garden yesterday—*and* that Grandma Mimi didn't buy all my "asking for a friend" stuff. I absolutely wasn't in the mood to talk to Mom about it right now. I couldn't handle Mom saying that I was still her little baby and she wasn't ready for me to grow up yet. The funny thing is, I actually *agree* with her. I *don't* feel ready to grow up. I made a mess of things *because* I'm not ready.

I was about to tell Mom that I had a stomachache and wanted to lie down... but Mom got this really weird look on her face.

Mom shifted from foot to foot. She looked like she was going to cry, which scared me. I walked back down the stairs, suddenly worried something was really wrong.

There were pink spots on Mom's cheeks. Her eyes were wet with tears. I felt a lump in my throat, too. Telly might have run away? He could be outside somewhere, *lost*?

Mom was right that Juice Box would be devastated . . . and she looked pretty devastated herself for not telling him yet. The day Telly possibly escaped, she'd gone upstairs with the twins before I even came down for breakfast . . . *and* before Juice Box realized Telly was gone. But Mom worried that the door had been open long enough for Telly to escape. Even though Dad assured her that it was very, very unlikely that had happened, Mom just had a terrible feeling.

Mom's chin trembled. She sank into a chair. I couldn't believe she was asking *me* for advice about what to do. How was I supposed to know? And also, it was always so strange to see adults make mistakes.

Finally, I went over to her and patted her arm.

And then I realized something: Mom and I are sort of in the same situation. She's scared to tell Juice Box about Telly because she doesn't want to break his heart and let him down. I'm scared to talk to Kristian because I don't want to break *his* heart and let *him* down. And we're both trying to protect other people's feelings by avoiding the truth. But as Mrs. Hines has told me, sometimes that's not good, because it means we don't look out for our *own* feelings, especially when we're bottling up things we need to say.

I thought of something else Mrs. Hines told me, too.

I'm not sure why I imagined Mrs. Hines on a cloud right then. I guess because people speaking on clouds seem very wise.

Anyway, I looked at Mom.

I told her yes. Juice Box would be upset, and she knew that already. But it would be okay.

Mom sighed and thanked me for listening. She said she felt better just talking it over with me. She also said this.

I was surprised. Especially because Mom wasn't *crying* about it. And you know what? I felt sort of grown-up, too. Mom had come to me for advice. She'd never really done that before!

And as I walked up to my room, things suddenly became clear. I needed to look out for my feelings, too. I needed to be okay with disappointing people. And I needed to save my friendships—before they were ruined forever.

I needed to tell the truth. Now.

PRETTY COOL

Dear Cosmo,

Just a few minutes later, Mom and I were in the car, driving to Kristian's house. Mom glanced at me in the rearview mirror.

I'd had to explain to Mom what was going on with Kristian, the Manners Party, the secret admirer note, and everything else. I didn't want to, but Kristian's house is too far away for me to walk or bike by myself. I had to ask Mom to drive me over, and she wanted to know why I needed to go so urgently.

So I told her. I'd braced myself for her reaction—she was either going to tell me to stop growing up *or*, on the total opposite side of the spectrum, she'd want to gossip about fifth-grade couples or even say that maybe I *should* like Kristian, because I was old enough for a first crush.

But surprisingly, Mom didn't say any of that. All she said was this.

I hoped so.

When we got to Kristian's, Mom said she was going to run to the pharmacy down the street and would be back in twenty minutes.

I watched her drive away, half wishing I could jump back in the car with her.

My heart raced as I walked up Kristian's front steps. My fingers shook as I rang his doorbell. I fiddled with Kristian's thank you note, which I'd put in my pocket when I decided to come over here.

Then I heard footsteps.

Kristian came outside. He looked so happy to see me. My throat felt raw. I couldn't get a full breath. But I had to be honest, Cosmo.

It felt like such a relief to say. Freeing, almost. But Kristian frowned.

Kristian's eyes got very wide.

He seemed like he had absolutely no idea what I was talking about. All of a sudden, I was afraid I'd made a huge mistake. Maybe I hadn't solved the mystery. Maybe the note *wasn't* from Kristian.

I reached into my pocket, pulled out Kristian's thank you note, and smoothed it out for him to see.

Kristian's cheeks were getting redder and redder. But then he started laughing. He pointed to the paper.

I stared at him. Then I turned the page over. That's when I realized.

Kristian's sentence *continued*. On the back.

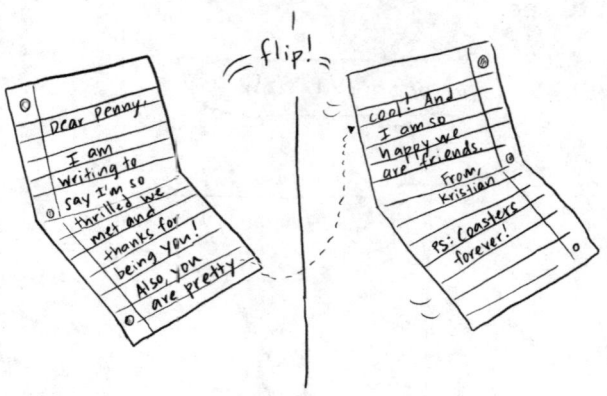

Oh. My. Goodness.

I couldn't believe it. How had I missed that? I was so annoyed at my brain for not thinking to flip the paper over sooner.

The worst part was that I was standing on Kristian's stoop, accusing him of having a crush on me—and he didn't!

I'd never felt so embarrassed.

Kristian was starting to put a few things together, too.

But Kristian said he was glad I finally *did* say something. He and the rest of my friends were really worried that something horrible was going on with me, something I could only tell Chloe.

Kristian also said something else.

I let out a huge sigh of relief.

I said I felt the same way. Well, I don't just want to ride coasters... but I got what Kristian meant. I just want to have fun. I don't want to be a teenager yet. I'm not ready to grow up.

And maybe I don't have to.

Kristian also made sure I knew something else.

Which, um, I guess was a compliment? So I thanked him.

Kristian also had this idea.

I smiled. It felt like too long of a story to explain that I'd actually had the same idea yesterday morning, but I immediately said yes. It was settled. I was going to the Manners Party with a friend after all.

We were still standing on Kristian's porch when Mom came back from the pharmacy. As she pulled up in front of the house, I gave her a big smile and wave, and she looked relieved. She yelled that she'd come back a little later to pick me up.

Then Kristian said this.

Which, of course, I did.

BLAH-LA

Dear Cosmo,

It was the day of the Manners Party, but I was much less nervous about it. Once I realized my mix-up with Kristian's thank you note, I got on the phone with all of my friends and explained everything. I felt a little embarrassed about admitting it, but my friends understood.

Everyone assured me that there definitely had been no fifth-grade memo of any kind. Not about crushes. Not about growing up. Not about any of it.

So there you go, Cosmo. We're all on the same page.

Well. Except for Chloe, who was helping us get ready for the party.

Chloe also said she had no idea I hadn't told all my other friends about my secret admirer note—if it had been *her*, she would have told everyone. She also apologized for sending me so many texts—she should have realized I felt sensitive about it. She should have backed off.

So anyway, the party was that night. And I have to say, I was excited. Especially once we all put on our fancy clothes.

Maria was also excited, but her excitement was the nervous kind. Turns out, she got 100 percent in her other manners class, the one about bed making, and she wanted to go two-for-two with our Manners Class as well. We kept reminding her that we weren't going to be graded on it . . . but, well, she was putting a lot of pressure on herself anyway.

We all headed to the community center where the party was taking place. A lot of kids were already there, waiting for the Winks to open the doors. Everyone seemed a little unsure about wearing fancy clothes.

Petra decided to show up to do some "light picketing" against traditional manners. I was surprised that Ursula was part of her protest line.

Before Mom left, she got some good goofy pictures of my friends and me.

Until this happened.

Madame Wink appeared out of nowhere! She seemed so annoyed that Mom hurried to her car. Petra left pretty fast after that, too.

The Winks unlocked the doors for the party and gave us some instructions.

And so we all filed into the ballroom. I have to say, it was *very* grown-up inside. There was fancy classical music playing on the stereo. There was all of *this*, too.

We were sad about not being able to touch or try chocolate from the chocolate waterfall.

I mean, what's the point of Willy Wonka-style chocolate if you can't eat it?

A lot of kids started toward the other treats right away, but Madame Wink was ready with her triangle.

Everyone sighed.

We tried to make things fun by pulling out each other's chairs—according to the Winks, pulling out chairs for people is *very* polite. Kristian pulled out my chair for me, so I pulled his out for him. Then I pulled out Rocco's, and he pulled out Maria's, and then Rocco's chair tipped over, and we all giggled.

But Maria shushed us.

Still, we tried to make the best of it. For a while, we all made polite chitchat. We passed around the bread basket from right to left and put our napkins in our laps. I thought we were being very grown-up. Also, the party didn't seem intimidating at all. If this was what a teenager-style party is all about, I can live with that.

After a few minutes, Mrs. Wink passed around some papers.

I couldn't believe it. A test at a party?

Mrs. Wink's test was fifty questions long. Some of them were really hard—how was I supposed to remember how many tines a seafood fork has? It took us all a while to finish. The only sounds in the room were the scratching of our pencils. Well, that and the plinkety-plink classical music playing in the background.

Finally, when I was done, I excused myself to the bathroom, carefully following Madame Wink's instructions for how to do so politely. News flash: You don't jump up and loudly announce you have to pee. You do *this*.

I thought the bathroom was empty, but after a moment, I heard someone's voice coming from the back corner.

There was a long pause. Then the stall door unlatched, and Riley came out. She didn't look happy.

Riley looked at me like she was going to say something snarky about me and my secret admirer, but then she seemed to change her mind and just let out a long sigh.

I couldn't believe what she said next.

I stared at her, confused. Hadn't Riley had a crush on Michael McMinnamin forever? I figured going on a date with him had been her idea!

I never imagined that Riley would be scared about this sort of thing, but I tried to keep my face neutral. I actually felt relieved. Maybe Mrs. Hines was right. Maybe most of us weren't ready for crushes—not really.

I realized Riley was still standing there, almost like she wanted me to say something. Then it occurred to me that she might be waiting for some advice. From *me*, of all people. Like I was some kind of expert! It was funny—she'd asked me for advice during the school play, too. And that made me wonder.

Did Riley . . . *look up to me*?

Nah. That idea was too weird.

But just in case, I tried to say something useful.

Wow. I couldn't believe Riley liked my suggestion.

Then she leaned closer.

Actually, Cosmo, I kind of agreed. This party *was* disappointing. I'd hyped it up so much in my mind, but everyone seemed so tense, and nothing exciting had happened.

Then I realized something. Does this mean being a teenager is . . . *horribly dull*? Do I have nothing but *boringness* to look forward to?

That doesn't sound fun at all.

THE BIRD

Dear Cosmo,

When I went back to the table, it seemed like Riley's attitude was catching. *Everyone* seemed restless and bored. Most people had abandoned their quizzes and were fiddling with their food. It also seemed like the same classical song was playing over and over.

Then Mrs. Wink put on a movie showing us the basics of the box step, one of the dances we'd be doing tonight. The problem was, it looked like the World's Most Boring Dance Ever.

No one really seemed excited about the fancy dances anymore. They definitely weren't paying attention to the video, which kept showing the same pair of feet over and over and made no sense.

Rocco looked really nervous about dancing. Maria tried to keep him calm.

The thing was, Rocco seemed sort of paralyzed.

The rest of us went to dance, but, well, it was kind of a disaster.

Most people stopped dancing quickly because of toe injuries, twisted ankles, or sudden needs to go to the bathroom, which I think was code for extreme embarrassment. Pretty soon, the only people remaining on the dance floor were Mr. Howdy and Ursula.

And it seemed like the more restless people got, the more Madame Wink critiqued.

She even criticized the chaperones.

Things went from bad to worse. Being fancy and polite was starting to stress *everyone* out.

And then this happened to Oliver during dessert.

We couldn't even laugh at him, because laughing isn't polite.

At the end of the meal, Maria politely excused herself, got up, and left the table. Except she didn't go to the bathroom. I found her here.

Then Mrs. Wink became very annoyed because she'd tallied the results of our quizzes.

I guess Madame Wink was also at her breaking point, because finally she turned to all of us and said this.

This was not the answer Madame Wink wanted. She looked like she might storm out.

It seemed like *everyone* was ready to storm out, actually.

And then, out of the corner of my eye, I noticed something zip past.

Wait. Was that...?

I have no idea how a bird had gotten into the building, but people sprang into action. Mrs. Wink held up the STOP side of her crossing guard sign, thinking the bird might be able to read it and stop . . . except it didn't work. Then Michael tried to catch it with his sport coat. Oliver and Luke leapt from their chairs and tried to shoo it out a window.

And Chelsea Wink, well, she did this.

Mrs. Wink lunged to catch the bird, but then it flapped away, sending her crashing into the table with all the food. She fell so hard that the table tipped over, and the food went flying to the floor. *That* made Madame Wink panic.

I've never seen someone do such a dramatic dive to save some weird French cookies. Madame Wink caught a few of the cookies, but as she regained her footing, she slipped on an olive and flew backward again.

Into this.

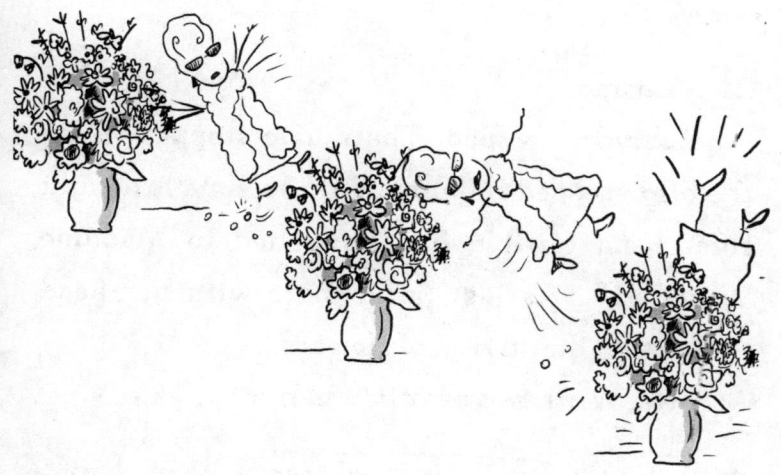

LIMBO TIME

Dear Cosmo,

Everyone gasped. The music stopped. Even the bird stopped flapping. For a minute I thought something terrible had happened to Madame Wink. She was just lying there with her head inside that giant vase of flowers.

Mrs. Wink ran over in a panic.

Mrs. Wink pulled Madame Wink out, and she seemed okay. I mean, she was covered in water and had a lot of twigs in her hair, but at least she was alive.

But she didn't look happy.

I felt sorry for Madame Wink, too. *All* the Winks, actually. They cared so much about this party, but it had been a huge disappointment—and maybe that was partly our fault. We'd failed our quizzes. We didn't have good enough manners. We were falling asleep in our slices of cake.

I guess everyone felt the same way I did, because we all stood up and slowly moved toward Mrs. Wink and her mom. And we all said this.

Mr. Howdy, Ursula, and a few of the boys jumped up to help Madame Wink back on her feet. Maria ran to get a towel to mop up Madame Wink's dress. Some of us tried to clean up the food that had fallen onto the floor, and Violet went over to comfort Chelsea in the corner. But Madame Wink still hadn't said a word. She had to be so, *so* mad.

But then this happened.

Wait. Was Madame Wink . . . *laughing*?

It was the most polite laugh I've ever heard.

Madame Wink kept laughing. Her *tee-hees* grew louder and louder until the twigs shook free from her hair. Then Mrs. Wink nervously laughed, too. So did Chelsea from her corner. And then we *all* laughed. Everything was so funny, suddenly. The food on the floor. Our fancy outfits. And the bird pecking at the remains of our elaborate feast.

The only person who didn't seem to be having fun yet was Maria. She'd come out of her hiding spot, but she still looked so stressed.

Maria looked over at who was talking. Madame Wink had overheard.

Everyone looked surprised that Madame Wink said that. Especially Maria.

Mrs. Wink looked a little embarrassed that she had just admitted that, but Madame Wink jumped in and said that it was true—every year, the Manners Party has always been a little . . . rowdy. Few fifth graders ever want to be as fancy as the Winks hope. Except Maria, apparently.

But Madame Wink also told Maria this.

That's really good advice for Maria. Maybe for all of us!

At that, Madame Wink went into the coat room, took off her fancy fur, and put on her normal fur again. That broke the ice. Suddenly, everyone else felt they could loosen up, too.

Kids helped themselves to a cake that hadn't fallen to the floor, and while they still used utensils, no one worried about using the wrong fork. Lulu threw chunks of her piece of cake to the bird, which kept hopping over to Chelsea. Chelsea was still scared of it, but she didn't seem *quite* as scared.

Kristian found the stereo and changed the music from the plinkety-plink classical stuff to the pop station on the radio. Then we all started dancing—*fun* dancing. Forget the box step or the foxtrot. And you know what? All of the Winks did, too. They were okay that we weren't doing proper steps. Madame Wink didn't even use her triangle. It was like falling into that plant had transformed her.

I can't say Rocco got any better at dancing, but it didn't really matter.

For the next hour, the party was really, *really* fun. But don't worry, Cosmo. We still tried to be polite here and there.

We just did it our way.

EPILOGUE

Dear Cosmo,

You'd think after that action-packed Manners Party we'd all be partied out for a while, but we had another party to attend the very next day. This one was the Way of Petra Party, which Mom said we could have at our house after all.

She'd told Juice Box about Telly, by the way. It was definitely hard.

Mom said she didn't know. She hoped not, but maybe. I felt awful for Juice Box—I know he felt a lot of disappointment and sadness. Mom squirmed, apologizing again and again that she'd left the door open *and* had taken so long to admit it. But I also think she felt better having told Juice Box the truth.

Everyone came to the party, including my friends, Riley, Violet, Lulu, Oliver, Michael, Luke, and even Ursula, Mr. Howdy, and Miss Kettle and Steve. And Chloe? Well, she came, too, and she brought a date.

Petra greeted us all at the door with some announcements.

I have to say, the rules got very silly.

Maria's rule was that we actually do one fancy thing: drink peppermint tea and eat these fancy little cakes she brought from her parents' restaurant. Mom had opened up our dining room table so that it sat a ton of people. I sat next to Kristian, and

Maria sat with Rocco, and Chloe sat with Devon, and Riley and Michael sat together. It looked like Riley had taken my advice about treating Michael like a friend, because they were giggling together and recapping yesterday's party.

After a series of brand-new rituals including greeting everyone with birdcalls, using toilet paper for napkins, and switching plates with the person next to you whenever someone said the word *pineapple*, we dug in to Maria's fancy desserts. Everyone was talking noisily, but it wasn't a big deal. One of the rules of the Way of Petra is that we can talk as loud as we want—but we have to let *everyone* tell their stories and not talk over people.

I looked around the table, watching everyone let other people talk and thinking about what Madame Wink said about how we'd shown true manners after she'd fallen into that vase. Then I realized something. Madame Wink's manners and the Way of Petra's manners aren't really that different. Manners might be all made up, but maybe we have them for a reason. They're all about kindness. Opening doors for people. Being sure not to say mean things. Using words of thanks, whether it's *thank you* or *gracias* or *mosquito*. Letting people talk, and making people feel included, and helping people up when they fall into giant vases of flowers or get trapped by birds.

They make us feel sort of safe. They give us a guide for what to expect. They're also kind of a map for what it takes to become a grown-up: being kind, considering others, trying your best, sometimes saying hard things, and sometimes, at least a little bit of the time, getting it totally wrong.

I guess I'd gotten something out of Manners Class after all.

As we ate, I thought I heard a strange sound in the corner of the dining room. I tried to ignore it, but then Rocco said this.

We all got quiet. There definitely was rustling. It got louder and louder. Everyone was on edge, afraid that an animal had gotten into the house or something. But then, suddenly, from a dark corner, *something emerged*.

Juice Box ran over to his tortoise, amazed and ecstatic. I couldn't believe it. I have no idea where Telly had come from or where he'd been hiding—we'd looked everywhere! What had made him come out now?

Everyone had a theory.

Whatever the case, Petra quickly came up with a new rule: Tortoises are special guests of honor at all Way of Petra events. And so we plopped Telly on a little pillow next to Juice Box and gave him a big piece of lettuce—which he chomped eagerly. I have to say, Telly made a very good surprise guest.

Then, after the party ended, a funny thing happened. I'd gone upstairs and seen that my friend Henry from New York wanted to video chat. I signed on, and I told him all about the Manners Party, the Way of Petra Party, Telly's reappearance, and even my secret admirer mix-up. It was fun to tell Henry everything, and he said he was so sad he couldn't be there, because all of it sounded like a wild, silly adventure.

But then, at the end of the call, Henry said this.

There was a period after *pretty*. This wasn't a sentence I needed to flip over to read the rest. Henry's voice cracked awkwardly. And he was blushing, suddenly . . . and he looked like he wanted to hang up kind of fast.

As I peered at Henry through the screen, I felt like blushing, too. Though . . . not in a bad way. Then some thoughts popped into my head: Henry's smile is so cute. He always has funny things to say. It's great how he always wants to listen.

So I said thank you. My voice cracked, too.

After we hung up, I sat on my bed for a minute, going over the thoughts I'd just had. I thought Henry's smile was cute. Did that mean I thought *Henry* was cute?

I felt surprised . . . but sort of *happily* surprised. Maybe I did have a crush—a little one. It didn't mean I had to do anything about it now. But maybe I will be ready for all that stuff someday. And maybe, when I am, it won't be scary at all.

And even if it is, I'll always have you, Cosmo. Every step of the way.

ACKNOWLEDGMENTS

I have been so lucky to spend six books with Penny. I've loved every moment of it, including seeing Penny slowly changing, learning, and growing up. It seems like every book in the Penny series is my favorite, and this one is no exception. Unlike Penny, I didn't take a manners class when I was in fifth grade, but my son Kristian (who, yes, is like the Kristian in this book, sort of!) did, which provided me with a lot of material for this story. Kristian's manners class didn't have nearly as much silliness, and the party certainly didn't end in disaster, but I do think the class taught him and his friends how to be polite and kind when interacting with others. (I also hope it was a little bit fun.)

I'm so grateful for the team that has supported me through the Penny journey. Writing this series has been a real dream, so words can't express how much it means that I actually got the chance to write and illustrate all of these novels. Big thanks to Jen Klonsky and Matt Phipps in Penguin Random House editorial and to Lanie Davis, Josh Bank, Romy Golan, and Les Morgenstein at Alloy. Thank you to Suki Boynton, Marikka Tamura, and Lily Malcom on the art side for juggling all the drawings and putting together the cover and the paperback designs. Thanks to Jordana Kulak, Christina Colangelo, Lauren Festa, and Alex Garber in marketing and publicity, as well as Ana Deboo in copyediting and Bethany Bryan, Rob Farren, Cindy Howle, and Misha Kydd in proofreading.

Thank you to all of the readers and schools who have supported me and allowed me to come into classrooms and libraries and talk about Penny and her worries. Thank you to the students of schools in Wardensville, Frederick, Tucson, Richmond, Louisville, Oakland, Houston,

Pittsburgh, Los Angeles, Philadelphia, and more for your excellent brainstorming about future books in the Penny series. My favorites continue to be "Penny Goes to the Moon" and "Penny Clones Herself."

And finally, thank you to my family—Michael, Kristian, and Henry, as well as the animals in my family: Bonnie, Clyde, Kitty, and Morris the tortoise, who was the inspiration for Telly and who also has gotten lost on several occasions. Glad we're always able to find you, buddy!

ABOUT THE AUTHOR

SARA SHEPARD is the author of the #1 *New York Times* bestselling series Pretty Little Liars, along with many other novels for young adults and adults. The Penny Draws series is her first one for younger readers. She lives in Pennsylvania with her husband, dogs, and sons Henry (who would have been named Penelope James had he been born a girl) and Kristian (who, like the character, loves all things roller coasters, especially riding them and talking about them).

The Penny Draws series is now available in paperback!